When I'm a
Big Bear

HiRE
S

/N
RY

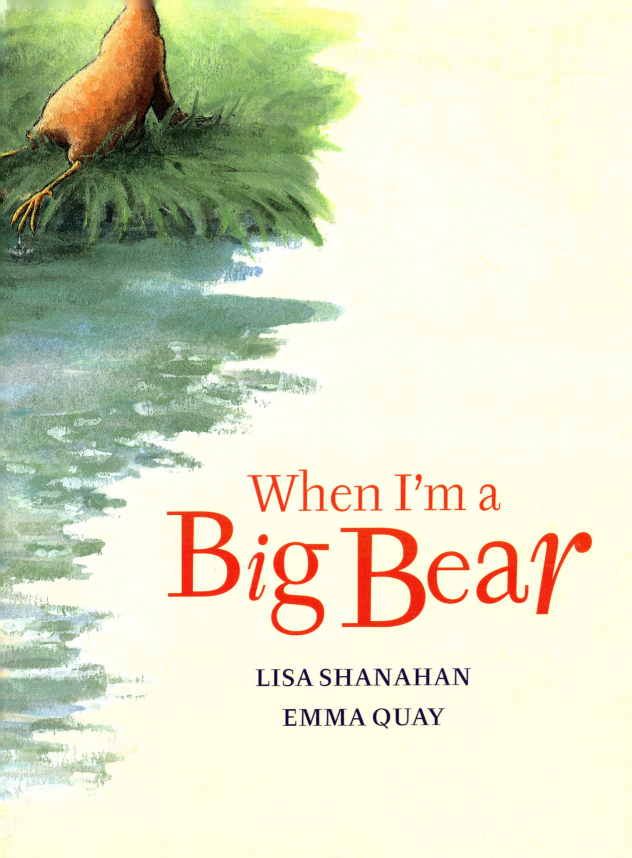

When I'm a
Big Bear

LISA SHANAHAN

EMMA QUAY

CAT'S Whiskers

THE WATTS PUBLISHING GROUP LTD

One morning Bear and Chicken sat by the pond,
watching the dragonflies skim and buzz.
'What do you want to be when you grow up?' asked Bear.
'An old chicken,' said Chicken.
'Oh,' said Bear, wrinkling his nose.
'What about you, Bear?' asked Chicken.
'I think,' said Bear, 'that when I'm a big bear
I'd like to be a builder.'

After breakfast, Bear and Chicken built a mud castle.
'I can see the sea,' cried Bear, waving from the turret.
'Careful up there,' called Chicken.
'And the mountains,' hollered Bear, climbing on the roof
and stretching tall, 'and the forest and the —'
'Watch out!' squawked Chicken.

The turret tipped.

CRicKeTy-
CROcK
SpLoDge

'It just missed you, Chicken,' cried Bear.

'By a wing,' shivered Chicken.

'I don't think I want to be a builder
when I'm a big bear,' said Bear.

'Good!' gasped Chicken.

'I wouldn't mind being an explorer, though.'

After morning tea, Bear and Chicken explored in the forest. They searched under stones and inside old trees. They found a slice of green glass and an old bike tyre.

'There's something down here,' said Bear, poking a stick down a deep hole.

'Watch out!' squawked Chicken.

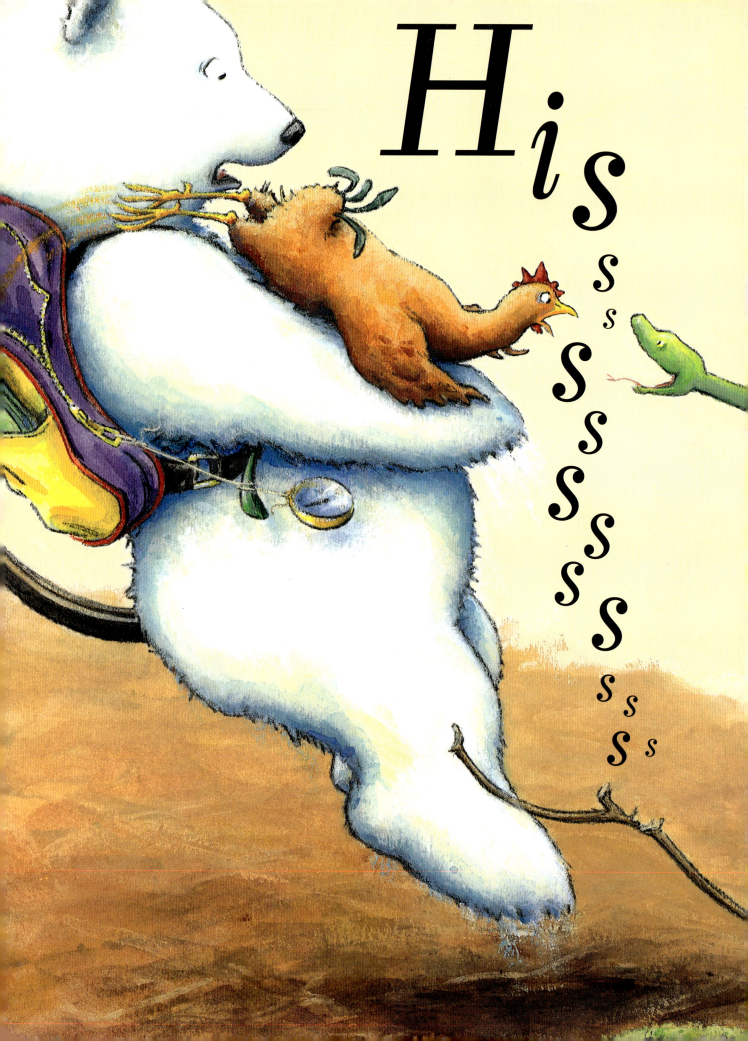

Hisssssss

Out snapped a snake.

'Run!' roared Bear. And they ran as fast as they could back to the pond.

'It just missed you, Chicken,' cried Bear.

'By a tail feather,' shivered Chicken.

'I don't think I want to be an explorer when I'm a big bear,' said Bear.

'Good!' panted Chicken.

'I wouldn't mind being a sea captain, though.'

After lunch, Bear and Chicken sailed across the pond.
Chicken took the helm while
Bear manned the cannon.
'Enemies above!' yelled Bear at a flock of seagulls.
He swung the cannon up. 'Ready... Aim...'
'Watch out!' squawked Chicken.

peeee-OOOOW!

VRRRRRRH!

PFFFFFFFFFF!

GLOB!

GLOB!

GLOB!

Water gushed over the deck.
'It just missed you, Chicken,' cried Bear.
'By a foot,' shivered Chicken.
'I don't think I want to be a sea captain
when I'm a big bear,' gurgled Bear.
'Good!' spluttered Chicken.
'I wouldn't mind being a pilot, though.'

When afternoon tea was over, Bear and Chicken
hoisted a plane to the top of the hill.
'Look at me! Look at me!' yelled Bear,
teetering on the crest of the runway.
'I'm looking,' called Chicken.
'Yee-haa! Whoo-hoo!' screamed Bear,
as he hurtled down.
'Watch out!' squawked Chicken.
'Duck!' bawled Bear.

Whooooosh
CRaCK

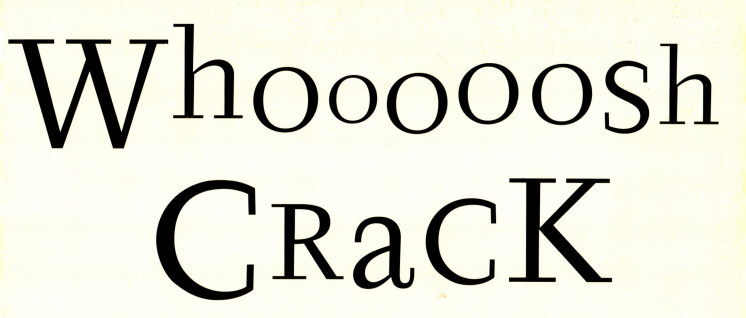

'It just missed you, Chicken,' cried Bear,
dusting off the dirt.

'By a beak,' shivered Chicken.

'I don't think I want to be a pilot
when I'm a big bear,' said Bear.

'Good!' whimpered Chicken.

'That does it,' said Bear. 'I need to try something new!'

'Why don't we be ... dancers?' asked Chicken.

'Excellent,' said Bear. 'Just the thing!'

After dinner, Bear and Chicken danced on a stage down by the pond.
Bear belly-danced while Chicken did the Cha-Cha.
'Isn't this fun!' said Chicken.

'Isn't this great!' said Bear, giving his belly an extra big bounce.

'Watch out!' squawked Chicken.

Smack

The backdrop and the wings and the stage collapsed.
Bear poked his head up through a hole. He gazed around.

'Chicken?' he called. 'Chicken? Chi-i-i-i-icken?'

Bear leapt to his feet. His heart thumped so hard that it hurt.
The wind whispered and the reeds rustled.

'CHICKEN?'

The frogs croaked and the crickets chirped.

'CHICKEN!' he wailed. 'Chicken! Where are you?'

'Here I am,' said a little voice.

Chicken slithered out from underneath the stage.

'Oh, Chicken! Thank heavens!' sobbed Bear.

'It just missed you!'

'By a claw,' shivered Chicken.

'I don't think I want to be a dancer

when I'm a big bear,' said Bear.

'Good,' whispered Chicken.

'I want to be just like you,' said Bear.

'An old chicken?' asked Chicken hopefully.

'No, silly,' said Bear. 'An old bear!'

That night, after supper, Bear and Chicken
lay by the pond and watched the moon.
'I wonder what it would be like to touch
the moon's skin,' said Bear.
'I wonder,' said Chicken, sleepily.
'Sometimes,' said Bear, 'I think I wouldn't mind
being an astronaut.'

Chicken sat up.

'Oh, Bear, please.

Let's wait until tomorrow!'

For Lynne and Monica
LS

For Sophie
EQ

This edition first published in 2002 by
Cat's Whiskers
96 Leonard Street
London EC2A 4XD

ISBN 1 903012 53 8 (hbk)
ISBN 1 903012 54 6 (pbk)

A Mark Macleod Book
Published in Australia and New Zealand in 2002
by Hodder Headline Australia Pty Limited

A CIP catalogue record is available from the British Library

Design by MATHEMATICS

Illustration technique:
black Lumograph pencil and acrylic paints on
Arches cold pressed watercolour paper

Printed in China